THERE'S A BEAR IN THE BATH!

NANETTE NEWMAN

THERE'S A
BEAR
IN THE BATH!

Illustrated by Michael Foreman

HARCOURT BRACE & COMPANY

San Diego   New York   London

Printed in Italy

First published in Great Britain in 1993
by Pavilion Books Limited

First United States edition 1994

Library of Congress Cataloging-in-Publication
Data available upon request
ISBN 0-15-285512-2

A B C D E

L<small>IZA</small> looked out the window and saw a bear sitting in the garden, so she went outside and asked, "What are you doing in my garden?"

"I'm here for a visit," said the bear.

"Why?" asked Liza.

"Why not?" replied the bear.

"I don't know," said Liza.

"Exactly," said the bear, "and by the way, when bears come to visit they usually get invited in."

"Oh, please come in," said Liza.

The bear looked around the kitchen.

"Would you like something to eat?" asked Liza."

"Like what?" asked the bear.

"Porridge," said Liza.

"What makes you think bears like porridge?"

"Well," said Liza, "when Goldilocks went to the three bears' house . . ."

"Oh, that," said the bear. "You didn't believe any of that, did you? Next you'll be saying that all bears like honey." He poured himself a cup of coffee.

"What's your name?" asked Liza.

"Jam," said the bear.

"Nobody is called Jam," said Liza.

"I am," said the bear.

"How come?" asked Liza.

"My mother," said the bear, helping himself to a cookie, "loved jam more than anything in the world—then she had me and she loved me more than anything in the world, so she called me Jam."

"I see," said Liza, not seeing at all. "It just seems like a funny name for a bear."

But the bear wasn't listening. He'd turned on the radio and was dancing and spilling potato chips everywhere.

He danced into the hall, twisting and twirling, and into the living room, and then lay down on the sofa.

"You're a good dancer," said Liza.

"I know," said the bear. He picked up a newspaper. "I'm brilliant at crossword puzzles," he said.

"That's showing off," said Liza.

"What is?" asked the bear.

"Boasting about how good you are at something," said Liza.

"Oh, no," said the bear, "boasting is very unattractive in a child, but boasting when you're a bear is quite acceptable."

"Really!" said Liza.

"Yes, really," said the bear. "Now, what is the word for something you can't stand—ten letters?"

"I don't know," said Liza.

"Unbearable," said the bear.

"That's brilliant," said Liza.

"Yes, I told you I was," said the bear, smiling.

He jumped up and started to dance again.

"I dance the tango best of all," he said.

"What's the tango?" asked Liza.

The bear took a rose from the vase, placed it between his teeth, grabbed Liza around the waist, and marched up and down the room, singing and leaping and swirling Liza around with him until she fell down in a breathless heap.

"Now that," said the bear, "was the tango. Of course, you have to practice a lot before you can do it as well as me. What's upstairs?" he asked, already on his way there.

"My room," said Liza, as the bear flung open the door.

"It needs trees," said the bear.

"Trees?" asked Liza.

"Definitely," said the bear. "A few big trees growing in here would give it style, make it more like a forest."

"But people don't have trees growing in their rooms," said Liza. "And who'd want to live in a forest?"

"Bears," said the bear, picking up Liza's school jacket. He tried to put it on and it split right down the middle.

"Badly made," said the bear, throwing it into the wastepaper basket.

"You were too big for it," said Liza, wondering what she'd wear to school on Monday.

"No, no," said the bear. "If a jacket doesn't fit a bear, there's something wrong with the jacket, not something wrong with the bear. Always remember that."

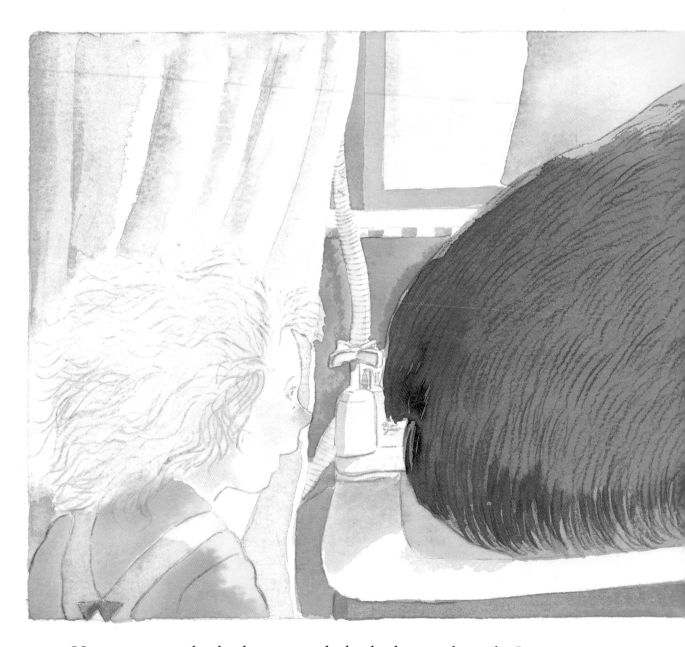

He went into the bathroom and climbed into the tub. It was a very tight fit.

"This tub is too small," said the bear.

"Well, it's big enough for me," said Liza.

"What's the use of that if it's not big enough for a bear?"

Just then, Liza heard her mother come in; she'd been chatting with their next-door neighbor.

"Time for dinner," she called upstairs.

"There's a bear in the bath!" shouted Liza.

"Is there, sweetheart? That's nice. What's his name?"

"Jam," yelled Liza.

"Oh, I forgot to get it. Never mind, I'll get some tomorrow." She started to set the table. Liza went back to the bathroom.

The bear was drinking shampoo and wearing frilly underwear on his head.

"How do I look?" he asked.

"You look like a bear with frilly underwear on his head," said Liza, but the bear had already disappeared into Liza's brother's room.

Jack was standing up in his crib, looking rosy from his nap.
"Teddy," he said, pointing at Jam and drooling with excitement.
"No! Jam," said the bear. "He's not very bright, is he?"
"Well, he's only two," said Liza.
"When I was two, I could count up to 1,104 and play the violin," said the bear, scooping Jack out of his crib.

Liza's mother called from downstairs, "Liza, have you finished your homework yet?"

"Mommy," shouted Liza, "there's a bear in Jack's room giving Jack a bear hug."

"That's nice," said her mother. "Tell Jack to say thank you."

"I think it's time to go," said the bear.

"Where to?" asked Liza.

"Oh, just somewhere," said the bear, vaguely. "I lead a very busy life, you know. I've got a singing lesson at four."

"I didn't know that bears sang," said Liza.

"Let's face it," said the bear, "you didn't know much at all about bears until you met me."

"That's true," said Liza.

"What will you do when I've gone?" asked the bear.

"I have to do my homework," said Liza. "I have to write about what I've done today."

"That's easy," said the bear. "Just write that you met this totally wonderful, clever, fascinating bear."

"No one would believe me," said Liza.

And they didn't!